Please retu
show
telephor

Northamp

www

First published in 2008
by Wayland

This paperback edition published in 2009

Wayland
338 Euston Road
London NW1 3BH

Wayland Australia
Level 17/207 Kent Street
Sydney, NSW 2000

Series Editor: Louise John
Editor: Katie Powell
Cover design: Paul Cherrill
Design: D.R.ink
Consultant: Shirley Bickler

A CIP catalogue record for this book is available from the British Library.

ISBN 9780750255301 (hbk)
ISBN 9780750255318 (pbk)

Printed in China

Wayland is a division of Hachette Children's Books,
an Hachette Livre UK Company

www.hachettelivre.co.uk

The Fun Race

Written by Pippa Goodhart
Illustrated by Sue Mason

WAYLAND

The class was getting dressed after PE.

Nasim gave Jake a poke. "Stop it!" said Jake.

Miss Samson was talking.
"I want you to get into
groups and make up some
races for sports day," she said.

Nasim gave Jake another poke.
"Stop it, Nasim!" said Jake.

"Jake! I heard you talking,"
said Miss Samson. "Stay and
tidy up, please."

"That's not fair, Miss! Nasim
was poking me!" said Jake.

Jake tidied up. In the cupboard, he found boxes full of ropes and hoops.

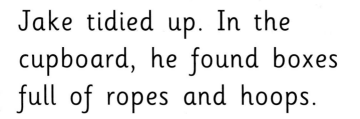

"I've got a good idea for a race," said Jake.

At lunchtime, Jake told Nasim
and Bella his idea.

"The race will have climbing and jumping and all sorts of things!" said Jake.

"Great!" said Bella and Nasim.

They drew a plan of the race.

"First, there will be ropes to climb," said Bella.

"Then there will be some cartwheels," said Nasim.

"And, to finish," said Bella, "jumping from hoop to hoop."

"Now for the best part," said Jake. He wrote something in very tiny writing on the bottom of the page.

They gave their plan to
Miss Samson.
"This looks good," she said.

On sports day, all the
children set up their races.

"That one looks fun," said Bella.

"It won't be as much fun as our race!" said Jake.

19

Miss Samson blew her whistle
and the races began.

There was a three-legged race.

Then a wheelbarrow race.

Then, it was Jake, Bella and Nasim's turn.

"Are you ready?" asked Miss Samson.

"No," said Bella. "This isn't a race for us."

"This is a race for the teachers!" said Jake.

"What?" said Miss Samson.

"It was on the plan!" said
Nasim, and he pointed to the
tiny writing. "Look!"

Everyone cheered as the teachers ran the fun race.

They swung from rope
to rope.

27

They did some cartwheels.

And, to finish, they jumped
from hoop to hoop.

And Jake, Bella and Nasim cheered the loudest of all when Miss Samson won!

START READING is a series of highly enjoyable books for beginner readers. **The books have been carefully graded to match the Book Bands widely used in schools.** This enables readers to be sure they choose books that match their own reading ability.

Look out for the Band colour on the book in our Start Reading logo.

The Bands are:

Pink Band 1

Red Band 2

Yellow Band 3

Blue Band 4

Green Band 5

Orange Band 6

Turquoise Band 7

Purple Band 8

Gold Band 9

START READING books can be read independently or shared with an adult. They promote the enjoyment of reading through satisfying stories supported by fun illustrations.

Pippa Goodhart lives with her husband, three daughters, a dog, a cat and four chickens who all leave interesting footprints on her floors. She found learning to read hard, but now loves reading, and writing, books.

Sue Mason grew up in East Sussex, surrounded by trees, eating crumpets. She illustrates from a happy little studio called The Chocolate Factory, which she shares with special friends. Sometimes they break from work to have a little dance around and eat cake.